Dark Whispers: Short tales of terror

Dark
Whispers
Short tales of terror

Carlos
Medrano

This is a work of fiction. Similarities to real people, places, or events are entirely coincidental.

DARK WHISPERS: SHORT TALES OF TERROR

First edition. September 30, 2023.
Copyright © Carlos Medrano
Written by Carlos MedranoPrologue

PROLOGUE

In the world of storytelling, there is power in conciseness. In the brevity of words lies the ability to create dark and enigmatic universes that evoke intense emotions and envelop readers in a whirlwind of fear and suspense. Short stories, in particular, possess the gift of distilling horror in its purest and most penetrating form, a fleeting yet unforgettable spark that etches itself into the mind and heart.

Here, within the pages of Dark Whispers: Short tales of terror, we invite you to delve into a world where every word counts, where the economy of language becomes a masterful tool to craft stories that will linger with you long after you've closed the book. From the first shiver to the final sigh, these tales will drag you into uncharted realms of imagination, where the inexplicable becomes tangible, and the unknown lurks in every corner.

In each micro tale, you will find the essence of primal fear, an ancestral instinct awakened by just a few sentences. Words become shadows that slink through your mind, creating vivid images that will make you doubt what you see and feel. From the dark corners of a room to the deepest recesses of the human soul, these short stories will unveil secrets, challenge your perceptions, and remind you that even in brevity, terror can be immensely powerful.

So, prepare to embark on this chilling journey. Open these pages with courage, but also with caution. For in Dark Whispers: Short tales of terror, you will discover how a complete story, full of emotions and entertainment, can be woven with just a few words.

Chapters

The makeup artist

The waiting line for the makeup session stretched for blocks. The best makeup artist, the comments on social media said, and women crowded the old shop, waiting for hours for the magic of the hands of a stranger who promised to transform them.

With his face inches from the eyes of an elderly woman, he finished giving the final touches of makeup before removing the latex gloves and a stained apron full of vermilion specks.

He hurriedly left and, just a few blocks away, rushed into the old beauty shop. He grabbed a stylist's smock and put it on quickly. He leaned over the woman waiting her turn and greeted her with a smile.

She widened her eyes upon seeing the pinned badge that read Funeral Makeup Artist.

Under the shade of the big cinnamon tree

The travelers had walked along long, tiring paths and looked into the distance, where they saw a tree with dense green leaves that blocked the intense rays of the sun.

A shade that promised respite for bodies that had endured scorching heat for many hours.

—Just a bit more, and we'll reach that shade, John— said the younger of the two with enthusiasm.

The older one raised his gaze and suddenly stopped in his tracks.

—What's wrong, John?— Asked the bewildered young man.

—That over there is a cinnamon tree, Matthew, and we can't rest in that place because beneath the cinnamon tree lies death.—

—Hahaha, nonsense,— Matthew laughed mockingly at old John.

—Believe me, it's better to continue our journey without stopping,—John warned Matthew, hoping his friend would see reason.

When they reached the tree, Matthew chose to stay, and John continued on his way.

The young man sat down, leaning his back against the rough trunk of the old cinnamon tree. He placed his straw hat over his face and let the breeze embrace him in the shade.

Three days later, John returned to the old cinnamon tree with a companion to look for his young friend.

There he sat, just as he had last seen him, with wide-open eyes and a pained expression on his face. In his right hand, you could still see drops of blood from the bite of a rattlesnake.

—I told you, boy!

The grandmother's necklace

Her name is Tina, a young woman who, along with her mother and grandmother, has been the talk of the town. During the last full moon of the year, the old woman had sworn never to leave them and had cast a spell on Mother Nature to bend to her will.

—I shall always be close to the heart, whether it be gold or silver that they wear— the old woman chanted into the wind.

Months later, the sky claimed the soul of the old woman, and the trio suffered a fracture. For days, the townsfolk heard the incessant and heart-wrenching cries of young Tina and her mother, until suddenly, laughter returned.

Ms. Paige, a nosy neighbor for years, enjoyed eavesdropping and pressing her large ear against walls to listen.

—Leave your grandmother in bed, Tina!—

—Do you like my necklace, Mom?—

—Do you like mine, Tina?—

The conversation sounded so illogical to Paige, who hadn't seen the old woman for months.

—Don't go out without your grandmother, Tina.—

Paige soon peeked out to see Tina leaving, umbrella in hand, but no other human being in sight. With the sale of necklaces, wealth had come their way, and every night Paige heard them talking about the grandmother. She decided to go from listening to observing.

She searched and searched for a crack in the wood until she found what she needed, and that night she would see what was really happening. While working on the necklaces, Paige saw the women with a jar on the table, and that was her surprise.

—Pass me the grandmother!— Tina said urgently to her mother. And the jar moved across the table, spilling ashes.

Many necklaces on the table, made of silver, gold, and crystal, all fulfilling the promise to make the grandmother immortal.

The Whisper

I walked faster and faster. Everything was eerily silent. Darkness enveloped every part of my body, and the damp breeze numbed my joints.

My clouded mind slowly began to have flashes of memories that put me back into the context of what was happening. The taste of iron from the blood oozing from my forehead and running down my face to the corner of my mouth distracted me on the path.

The beats of my heart and the sound of my breathing were like revealing screams of my location with every step I took.

Now I remember. This forest was my choice for camping alone, but I was never alone. A cup of coffee by the campfire. One last sip and a whisper that said:

—I found you.—

The Sofa

His little feet traversed the hallway, dodging the toys he had scattered himself.

He crossed several doors, several rooms, until he reached the large living room where the old reclining sofa awaited him.

Mumbling and with a big smile, he hugged it for a few seconds, then turned around and ran away.

The sofa still had a thick, brown-toned scarf draped over its backrest. A cane rested on one side, and on the small tea table, the portrait of the grandfather rested on the sofa, caressing the head of the little one who returned every day to greet, smile, and flee.

The last goodbye

She was so angry and sad, walking from one room to another, haphazardly packing the last garments into the suitcase.

—Mom, don't leave me! I promise to behave,— the little boy pleaded through tears, stumbling and knocking over a photo that sat on the nightstand.

Amidst sobs, she carefully placed the picture back in its spot. She grabbed a baseball cap, and it was the last thing she packed in the suitcase.-

-Mom... Mom,— the child repeated, seated and huddled in the corner of the room.

Standing at the doorway, she turned and gazed intently at the small bloodstains that still remained on the torn carpet. And on the bed, the headline from the local newspaper from months ago that read, Child Loses Life While Handling Father's Gun.

The silent shadow in the mirror

Daniela never expected to inherit her grandmother's fortune. The mansion, covered in wisteria with lilac flowers, accentuated its architectural beauty. Of everything, only her grandmother's mirror remained. The sale of the mansion provided her with enough money to live this and another life.

Daniela soon forgot about the mansion, and as she settled the last books in her new home, she remembered that she still needed to decide where to place her grandmother's old mirror. Sitting on the wooden floor, she looked up and caught a glimpse of a shadow in the mirror's reflection from the corner of her eye. At that moment, she remembered when her grandmother used to sit her on her lap in front of the mirror, and they would both gaze into it while her grandmother brushed her white hair with an old, natural-bristle brush.

Almost hypnotized by the memory, she crawled closer to the mirror and sat down to contemplate the image it reflected that night. Once again, the shadow she had seen out of the corner of her eye a few minutes ago was there, but this time she paid closer attention.

—I love this mirror so much, Grandma!—

—It will be yours when I'm no longer here, but you must remember that it should only be here. Promise me you will never move it.—

A promise forgotten by Daniela and remembered at that moment by the silent shadow in the mirror. Her body suddenly trembled as she saw repressed memories of her life with her old witch of a grandmother flash before her in an instant. To her, Snow White was not just a Brothers Grimm fairy tale but something very real and chilling that time had buried deep within her memory.

Now she could hear her grandmother's warning about the mirror again. About the hidden door behind the reflection and the demons that dwell beyond the glass, waiting for the moment to take anyone who stands in front of it if it is moved from its place. Daniela opened her eyes wide and jumped to her feet to find something to cover the mirror. A white sheet at the foot of the bed seemed to be waiting for Daniela's hands. She hurried to her bed and yanked the white sheet. When she turned around, she stared at the mirror with the sheet in her hands and the silhouette of a shadow behind it.

The bedroom door opened, and Daniela's father appeared with a dinner tray in his hands. The room was empty. The sheet lay on the floor at the foot of the bed.

—Dad, Dad...—

The man picked up the sheet, and Daniela, from inside the mirror, saw as if a veil darkened the place where she now was, unable to escape.

Footsteps in the basement

It took Roberto's family just over a month to move into the old house his mother had managed to acquire with her life savings. It was a winter weekend, and despite the intense cold, the moving work was essential for the family who would spend the night in the living room, lying on old blankets that had managed to escape from storage boxes. Roberto was just a 15-year-old teenager who helped his mother take care of his younger siblings, aged 7 and 10. Their father was not spoken of; he had abandoned their mother a month ago after they had signed the purchase of the old house.

—Kids, it's time to sleep; there's still a lot of work to do tomorrow,— Roberto's mother shouted from the room adjacent to the living room. They all lay down on the floor and closed their eyes.

A strange noise woke Roberto up past midnight. A tapping that echoed in an still-empty house.

—Mom, do you hear that?— Roberto's mother got up quickly and grabbed the fireplace poker. The rest of the children opened their eyes and asked, still half asleep, what was happening.

—Mom, the noise is coming from the basement. It seems like someone broke into the house,—Roberto said, frightened.

—All right, stay here. I'm going down, and if you hear me scream, run out to alert the neighbors,—the brave lady said as she opened the basement door and began to descend. The noise grew louder as she descended the stairs. Upon reaching the last step, the moonlight filtering through the basement windows illuminated a ladder lying on the floor. She heard the tapping again and looked up to see her husband, who had disappeared a month ago, hanging from a wooden beam.

The song of the broken doll

Elia was delighted with the broken doll she found that afternoon in her grandmother's attic. It was a rag doll with a porcelain head and cotton hair. The string on her back still had the plastic ring that could be pulled to make her talk and sing.

At 8 years old, Elia was a child who loved running and playing all around the house, and her discovery excited her greatly. She couldn't resist finding out if the broken doll could still sing, so she pulled the string hard. As soon as she let go of the string, the broken doll began to sing, and to the rhythm of her song, Elia saw how the attic door closed.

She pulled the string again, and everything started to shake. Frightened, Elia left the doll and ran toward the door to exit the place, but she couldn't open it. She began to peer out of the windows, screaming and banging. No one could hear her. In her desperation, she stomped on the doll, and everything went dark. She stomped again and heard the porcelain head shattering into pieces. The song of the broken doll slowly faded, along with the unsettling events that had disturbed Elia for several minutes. She fell to her knees in exhaustion and, sobbing, saw the attic door swing open. Her grandmother hurried in and hugged her.

—Don't cry, dear. In the trunk, I have another doll just like this one,— Elia opened her eyes wide, let go of her grandmother, and ran out of the attic without looking back.

The last train at midnight

The rain beat insistently against the windows as a group of passengers gathered at the deserted train station. The clock on the tower struck midnight exactly when a flash of light pierced the darkness. The train's bell tinkled, and its doors slowly opened, inviting passengers aboard.

The carriage was illuminated by a dim yellow light, casting unsettling shadows in the corners. A shiver ran down Eleanor's spine as she entered and settled into a red velvet seat. Next to her, an elderly man with a wide-brimmed hat muttered to himself.

—I'm not sure if this train was a good idea, —the man said, looking around suspiciously. Eleanor nodded in agreement.

—It's strange, isn't it? It only runs at midnight, and there are no other passengers.—

The train began to move with a soft squeak of the rails, and the gentle swaying filled the carriage. Soon, passengers realized that the windows only showed impenetrable darkness, with no signs of the city or the outside world.

A nervous young man sitting across from Eleanor broke the silence. —Does anyone know where we're headed?— The man in the hat glanced out the window and frowned. —I have no idea. But something tells me this is not a normal journey.—

As the train continued, passengers noticed that time seemed to behave strangely. Minutes stretched and shrank as if time itself were distorted. The conversation grew anxious as they tried to make sense of the situation. —This is like a strange dream,—Eleanor murmured, looking around uneasily.

The nervous young man got up from his seat and walked to the carriage door. He tried to open it, but it was firmly closed. — We can't get out! We're trapped!— The man in the hat calmly got up and approached the young man. —The key here is to stay calm. There's something bigger at play that we don't yet understand.—

The carriage started to shake and jolt violently. Lights flickered, and a freezing cold filled the space. The floor seemed to wobble, and passengers clung to their seats, filled with fear. —This can't be real! —the young man exclaimed, holding onto a railing.

Amidst the chaos, Eleanor noticed a shadowy figure at the end of the carriage. It was a hooded figure slowly advancing toward them. —Look!—she whispered, pointing with a trembling finger.

The man in the hat stood up, facing the figure. —We cannot escape whatever is happening. We must face it together.—

The hooded figure raised its head, revealing bright eyes and a sinister smile. —Welcome to the midnight train, where secrets and fears come to life,—it said with a voice that echoed through the train's corridors.

The train shook more violently as passengers clung to the crumbling reality around them. They would confront their deepest fears before the final destination of the midnight train was fully revealed.

The curse of the hunted mirror

T he auction room was illuminated by a dim light that highlighted the objects on display. Among various antique items, an old mirror with an ornate frame caught the attention of those present. Its silvery surface seemed to hide centuries-old secrets.

At the back of the room, Emily, a young and ambitious collector, joined her friend Lucas, a hardened skeptic. Both observed the mirror with curiosity. —What do you think, Lucas? It's magnificent, isn't it?— commented Emily as she admired the mirror. Lucas shrugged. —It's just an old mirror. I don't understand why people get so excited about these things.— Emily smiled and gave him a challenging look. —Don't you believe in the possibility that something has history? Imagine what secrets this mirror might have witnessed. —

Finally, the auctioneer's hammer fell, and the mirror was awarded to Emily. She took the mirror to her home and placed it in her bedroom, facing the bed. As night fell, the room's shadows mingled with the moonlight streaming in through the window.

Once alone in the room, Emily approached the mirror. She looked at herself, but her reflection began to distort. She saw fleeting images of a woman in an old-fashioned dress, struggling to escape a raging fire. Horrified, she stepped back from the mirror and rubbed her eyes, attributing the visions to fatigue. However, the image persisted in her mind.

The next day, Emily invited Lucas to her house to share her experience. —Lucas, something strange is happening with this mirror. Last night, I saw a terrifying vision, as if I were looking into the past.—

Lucas raised a skeptical eyebrow. —Don't tell me you believe in all those urban legends about cursed objects.— Emily sighed, frustrated. —I don't know what it is, but I want to investigate it further. I need to understand why I saw those images.—

Together, they researched the mirror's history. They discovered that it belonged to a wealthy family from the 19th century who had lost their daughter in a tragic fire. The mirror had been in the young girl's room and had witnessed the horror of that fateful night.

As they delved deeper into the history, Lucas began to feel a chill down his spine. —It's just a coincidence, right? It can't have real power.—

Emily approached the mirror once more and gazed at her own reflection. This time, she saw Lucas in her visions, struggling to breathe in a smoke-filled environment. She turned to him, her eyes filled with concern. —Lucas, I've seen your fate in the mirror too!—

Lucas looked at her incredulously, but fear gripped him when he saw his own reflection distort in the mirror, revealing a vision of his tragic fate.

Together, Emily and Lucas continued their investigation, seeking a way to break the dark bond that the mirror had woven between them and their future. Along the way, they uncovered buried secrets, revealing the truth behind the family tragedy and how it had become trapped in the mirror.

With bravery, they faced their destiny and managed to free themselves from the power of the ancient mirror. As the visions disappeared, the mirror lost its ominous glow.

The experience changed Emily and Lucas forever, leaving them with a lesson about the power of forgotten stories and objects that hold their secrets. Now, the mirror rested in a dark corner of a museum, where its tragic history awaited rediscovery by future generations.

The forest of eternal shadows

The remote forest was shrouded in perpetual mystery, its tall, dense trees blocking out much of the sunlight. A group of four hikers, consisting of Alex, Mia, Jake, and Emma, bravely ventured into this silent realm.

As they advanced through the dense forest, the sun dipped below the horizon, and shadows began to lengthen, weaving a tapestry of darkness in their path.

The trees seemed to take on a life of their own, their branches creaking, and their leaves whispering secrets in the wind.

—Does anyone else feel like we're being watched?—asked Mia, nervously glancing around. Jake chuckled. —It's just your imagination, Mia. This forest may seem eerie, but there's nothing to fear.— But the laughter soon faded as the shadows started to move eerily.

As they ventured deeper into the forest, the shadows seemed to come alive, silently gliding between the trees and sliding along the ground.

—What's happening here?—asked Emma, her voice trembling. Alex raised his flashlight, trying to dispel the unsettling darkness.

—I don't know, but it seems like the shadows are... changing.— In the heart of the forest, the shadows grew darker and denser. The flashlights could barely penetrate the blackness that surrounded them. Suddenly, a larger and more grotesque shadow emerged among the trees.

—Run!—shouted Jake, and the group began to sprint through the dense forest, pursued by the shadows that seemed to creep up behind them. Laughter from earlier turned into screams of terror as the shadows closed in on them.

The forest became a dark and claustrophobic maze, and the feeling of being chased became more intense.

—We can't go on like this! We need to find a way out!— exclaimed Alex, trying to stay calm. Finally, they emerged into a small clearing illuminated by the moon. The shadows seemed to slow their advance, stopping at the edges of the clearing as if they were restrained by some invisible barrier.

—What... what did we just experience?— asked Mia, panting.

—I've never seen anything like it in my life,—admitted Emma, still trembling.

The shadows at the edge of the clearing seemed to recede slowly, as if the forest were regaining its tranquility. The group looked at each other, their expressions filled with disbelief.

—Maybe this forest has secrets we shouldn't disturb,—suggested Jake, his tone now more serious. Together, the hikers returned to their camp, carrying with them the terrifying memory of shadows coming to life in the forest's darkness. Although they couldn't explain what they had experienced, they knew they had witnessed something far beyond their understanding, a dark and ancient truth that only the remote forest held.

The mystery of the abandoned house

Deep within a quiet village stood an old, abandoned house. No one had entered it for years due to the stories circulating about its dark past. However, Lucas, a curious boy with bright eyes, couldn't resist the temptation to uncover the secrets it held.

One sunny day, Lucas approached the house with a mixture of excitement and apprehension. The door was ajar, creaky and weathered by time. He took a deep breath and, with a hesitant step, crossed the threshold. The interior was shrouded in shadows, the furniture covered in dust as silent witnesses of times gone by. Lucas ventured further inside, guided by his curiosity. As he explored, he found framed photographs depicting a smiling family: a couple and their young daughter.

—What happened to them?— Lucas wondered aloud, examining the photos. A soft, distant voice responded from the shadows.

—Their story is a sad one, young explorer. — Lucas turned, surprised. Before him materialized a translucent figure. It was a girl his age, dressed in clothing from the past century.

—Who are you?— Lucas asked, feeling a chill run down his spine. —I am Eliza,— the ghostly girl replied. —This house used to be my home. My family disappeared long ago, and their memories remained behind in this house.— Lucas felt a mix of fear and compassion for Eliza. —What happened to them? Why did they disappear?— Eliza sighed, her ethereal figure seeming to tremble.

—One day, a mysterious illness came to the village. My family fell ill, and they couldn't survive. People were so afraid of the disease that no one dared to enter this house after we left.— Lucas looked around, taking in the story.

—Are you still here because you couldn't cross over to the other side?— Eliza nodded sadly. —Yes, it seems I am trapped here, bound to these memories. But you have brought me a ray of hope, Lucas.

Perhaps, if you uncover what really happened, I can finally rest in peace.— As Lucas continued to explore the house, he found clues that revealed the family's desperate efforts to protect themselves from the illness. He also found a diary that spoke of their struggle to survive.

—Eliza, I've found the diary. Your family did everything they could to stay safe,— Lucas said, excited. Eliza's figure seemed to briefly shine.

—Thank you, Lucas. Now I can leave this house behind and reunite with my family. — As the shadows in the house faded, Lucas felt a comforting warmth. Eliza smiled and thanked him before disappearing into the light. When Lucas stepped out of the house, the sun shone on his face. He had uncovered a sad story and helped a spirit find peace. From then on, the abandoned house would no longer be just a place of darkness but a reminder of how an act of curiosity could change the fate of someone trapped between the past and the present.

The whisper of the night wind

In the quiet village of Willowbrook, life flowed peacefully, surrounded by green landscapes and clear skies. However, one day everything changed when an unusual wind began to blow from the east. It was no ordinary wind; it carried with it unintelligible whispers that filled the air with mystery.

In the village square, a group of neighbors gathered to discuss the strange phenomenon. —Have you felt that strange wind, Sarah?— asked Tom, a local farmer, of his neighbor. Sarah nodded, concerned.

—Yes, and the whispers it brings... I can't understand what they're saying, but they give me the creeps.— As the wind persisted, the inhabitants of Willowbrook began to show signs of unease. Their glances were furtive, and whispers in the streets multiplied. Nights grew darker, and nightmares began to afflict the sleepers.

In the carpentry workshop, David and Samuel discussed their own experiences with the wind.—Have you noticed how everyone is acting strangely?— asked David, nailing a piece of wood. Samuel nodded and sighed. —I've heard rumors that the wind is bringing dark secrets with it, driving people mad.— One night, as the wind howled in the streets, the inhabitants of Willowbrook gathered in the square once more, this time with desperate looks. —Something is wrong here,— said Emily, a local teacher. —People are becoming aggressive, as if something is tormenting them from within.— Tom stepped forward, fear in his eyes. —I've heard that these whispers are voices from the past, whispers of secrets buried beneath the soil of our village.— Tensions escalated, and disputes became common.

The tranquility that once defined Willowbrook faded amid confusion and paranoia. One day, as the wind roared louder than ever, Sarah ran to the square, her eyes filled with terror. —The secrets are coming to light! They're revealing everything we've hidden!—

The unintelligible voices of the wind began to take shape, forming clear phrases and words in the minds of the inhabitants. Secrets, betrayals, and dark deeds that had remained hidden for years were revealed to the world. Madness gripped the town as people struggled to confront the truth of their past.

Willowbrook, once an idyllic place, descended into chaos. The inhabitants gathered one last time in the square, with desperate and tormented faces. —This is our punishment for our sins,— murmured Samuel, looking around with glassy eyes. The wind continued to blow, carrying with it the voices of the revealed secrets. The inhabitants of Willowbrook faced the cruel reality that their dark secrets had come to life, consuming them from within. And so, the wind of whispers left its indelible mark on the village, turning its tranquility into a distant memory of a time when ignorance was a blessing.

The shadow game

On a stormy night, a group of friends, consisting of Alex, Maya, Jordan, and Lily, decided to challenge the darkness by venturing into an old abandoned house. Armed with flashlights and a mix of excitement and nervousness, they ventured into a place where echoes of the past seemed to resonate.

The house was shrouded in darkness and whispers as the friends cautiously explored the rooms. Finally, they reached a large hall, their flashlights creating dancing shadows on the walls. —What a perfect place to play the shadow game!— exclaimed Jordan, with a mischievous smile.

—Really? Here?— Maya asked, looking around with some apprehension. Lily laughed. —Come on, Maya, it's just a fun game. What could go wrong?— Alex nodded, trying to keep the mood light. —Exactly. We only need our flashlights and our hands to create interesting shadows.—

The friends sat in a circle, their flashlights pointing toward the center.

With their hands and flashlights in motion, shadows began to dance on the walls, forming strange and whimsical figures. However, as they continued, the shadows began to change shape on their own. Shadowy hands seemed to slide across the wall, creating silhouettes that the friends had not created. —Are you seeing this?— Maya whispered, her voice trembling. —It's just your imagination,— Alex tried to reassure them, but his own voice reflected his unease. The shadows seemed to move with a life of their own, departing from the innocent shapes they had attempted to create. They twisted into distorted and menacing forms. —I think we should stop this,— Lily suggested, her voice now full of nervousness.

But before they could move, the shadows began to converge in a corner of the room, forming a dark and ominous figure rising in the darkness. —I didn't do this!— Jordan exclaimed, stepping back. The shadowy figure advanced toward them, emitting a chilling unintelligible whisper. The flashlights began to flicker, and the light grew dimmer. —We have to get out of here!— Alex shouted, but his words seemed to be absorbed by the growing darkness.

The friends fled in panic, their flashlights barely lighting the way. The old house seemed to twist and groan around them as they struggled to escape the shadows that pursued them. Finally, they managed to exit the house, panting and terrified. Behind them, the shadowy figure seemed to fade into the storm, but its presence left an indelible mark on their minds. As the storm subsided and daylight returned, the friends looked at each other with eyes filled with wonder and fear.

—I think we should never have played with the shadows,— Lily murmured, her voice filled with warning. The shadow game had taken a dark and terrifying turn, reminding them that in the darkness of the night and in the depths of imagination, shadows could take on a life of their own, revealing an unknown and frightening side of the world they had believed they knew.

The specter in the rearview mirror

It was a dark and rainy night as Mark drove alone down a desolate road. His car's headlights barely pierced the dense fog that enveloped the path. His hands gripped the steering wheel tightly as he struggled to maintain control in the challenging conditions.

Suddenly, a flash of light blinded him, and a car appeared out of nowhere. Mark attempted to brake and steer, but it was too late. The sound of impact filled the air, and his world went black.

When Mark regained consciousness, he was dazed and injured in his wrecked car. He looked into the rearview mirror, and what he saw took his breath away: a terrifying specter with vacant eyes and an expression of rage stared back at him from the backseat. —It can't be real,— Mark muttered to himself, his voice trembling.

The specter in the mirror seemed to grin sinisterly before fading away. Mark staggered out of the car and crawled off the road, seeking help.

Hours later, the police and paramedics arrived at the scene. Mark was in shock, unable to explain what he had seen in the rearview mirror. Officers took his statement and assured him that there was no evidence of any specter.

When they finally let him go, Mark decided to head home. Every time he glanced into the rearview mirror, he felt a shiver down his spine. But there was no trace of the specter. —I must be imagining it,— he told himself repeatedly, trying to reassure himself.

Days passed, and Mark attempted to return to normalcy. However, whenever he drove, he had the uncomfortable sensation that something was watching him from the backseat. No matter where he looked, he saw nothing out of the ordinary.

One night, while driving alone on the same dark road, Mark saw a flash of light in his rearview mirror. He looked, and there it was again, the specter, staring at him with cold, hungry eyes. —You can't keep running,— the specter whispered in a voice that seemed to crawl through his mind.

Mark accelerated, trying to escape the specter that seemed to pursue him no matter how hard he tried to get away. The rain fell relentlessly as the car's headlights illuminated the deserted road. —Stop!— Mark yelled, his voice filled with desperation.

The specter only smiled and continued to follow him, its twisted and terrifying figure in the mirror.

Finally, Mark lost control of the car and crashed into a tree. As darkness enveloped him, he looked into the rearview mirror and saw the specter slowly approaching. — Your time has come,— the specter whispered before everything turned black.

The road remained deserted and silent, as if nothing had ever happened. Only the shattered remains of the car and an inexplicable mystery remained. The specter, finally satisfied, faded into the night, leaving behind a trail of horror and an unanswered question: who was the specter, and why did it relentlessly pursue Mark?

Whispers from beyond the grave

The mansion stood majestically in the middle of the countryside, surrounded by ancient trees and an air of mystery. The Turner family, consisting of Mark, Emily, and their young daughter Sophie, moved to the mansion in search of a fresh start. However, they soon discovered they were not alone.

On their first night in the mansion, while having dinner in the dining room, Emily furrowed her brow. —Did you hear that?— Mark looked up, puzzled.

—Hear what?—

—A whisper,— Emily said, her voice barely a whisper itself. Sophie, who was coloring at the table, looked around with wide eyes.

—I heard something too, Mom.— Mark chuckled softly. —It must be just the normal sounds of an old house. There's nothing to worry about.— But as the days passed, the whispers became more frequent, and the shadowy movements on the walls grew more prominent.

One night, as they prepared for bed, Emily saw a shadowy figure-shaped shadow glide down the hallway. —Mark, there's someone in the house!— Emily exclaimed, gripping his arm tightly. Mark quickly got up and turned on the light. — There's no one here, Emily. You must be imagining things.— But Emily wasn't convinced. The next morning, as she researched the history of the mansion at the local library, she discovered that the family who had lived there decades ago had vanished under mysterious circumstances. Mark joined her in the library, peering over her shoulder.

—What have you found?—

—The family that lived here before us disappeared without a trace,— Emily said, her voice tense.

—And there are rumors of strange occurrences in this house.— Sophie entered the room, rubbing her eyes.

—Mom, last night I saw a shadow in my room.— Tension in the room grew as Mark and Emily exchanged worried glances.

They decided to investigate further and, with the help of a local parapsychologist, uncovered that the former inhabitants of the mansion had been involved in occult practices and had mysteriously disappeared after a ritual gone wrong. One night, while they were together in the living room, the whispers and shadows intensified. A dark figure emerged from the shadows, moving toward them.

—We should not be here!— Emily screamed, trembling with fear. The figure materialized, revealing the spirit of one of the former inhabitants. —You've released us from our torment. Thank you.— With the parapsychologist mediating, the Turners helped the spirits find peace by solving the mystery of their disappearance. As the spirits faded into the darkness, the whispers and shadows began to fade as well. —We can finally be at peace,— Mark murmured, embracing Emily and Sophie. As the sun rose over the mansion, the Turners felt that the old house was filled with a new serenity, one it

had earned after years of secrets and
hardships. Now, the mansion became a
home for them, full of stories from the
past but also a future filled with hope.

The phantom reflection

In the most remote corner of her grandmother's old mansion, Amelia discovered a mirror intricately carved with exquisite details. Its golden frames gave it an air of mystery and charm. When the moonlight touched its surface, Amelia could swear she saw a fleeting glimmer of movement in its reflection. However, it was the dark shadows at its edges that truly intrigued her.

One night, while rummaging through her grandmother's attic for memories, Amelia found an old diary. Its yellowed pages revealed the story of a girl named Eliza, who had been her grandmother's friend when they were young. Eliza had mysteriously disappeared in the house at a young age.

Intrigued, Amelia decided to seek more information about Eliza. She scoured archives, spoke to elders in the village, and eventually found an elderly woman who remembered Eliza and how she had vanished in the house.

Determined to unravel the mystery, Amelia returned to the mirror and gazed into it. "If you're here, Eliza, show me what happened."

The reflection in the mirror shifted slowly. Instead of her own reflection, Amelia saw an old room with peeling walls and dusty furniture. A girl in a white dress, whose image was blurry and almost ethereal, stood in the center.

—Eliza— Amelia whispered, astonished.

The girl in the mirror seemed to turn toward her, her dark eyes filled with sadness. Amelia could feel the sorrow and longing emanating from her gaze.

—How can I help you, Eliza? Why are you trapped here?— Amelia asked aloud.

Eliza's image appeared to try to communicate but could only emit an unintelligible whisper.

Inspired by the need to set Eliza free, Amelia delved deeper into the history of the house. She discovered that Eliza had tragically died in an accident in the room she had seen in the mirror. As she uncovered more details, she realized that

Eliza had become trapped between the world of the living and the dead due to the injustice she had suffered in her short life.

One night, Amelia stood before the mirror and spoke aloud. —Eliza, I know you're here. Listen, I've found out what happened, and I'm here to help you find peace.—

Eliza's reflection in the mirror seemed to glow with a soft, warm light. Amelia felt a faint breeze, like a whisper of gratitude, before Eliza's image slowly faded away.

The room filled with silence, and Amelia knew that Eliza had finally found the peace she had longed for. With a sense of satisfaction and resolution, Amelia closed the diary and smiled.

The mirror, once a silent witness to a forgotten tragedy, was now filled with history and redemption. And Amelia, with her determination and empathy, had restored the balance between the worlds of the living and the dead, bringing peace to a tormented spirit.

The house of lost souls

The abandoned house, nestled on the outskirts of the village, was known for its history of death and tragedy. Despite the warnings and rumors, a group of friends decided to defy fate and spend the night there. The full moon shone down on the worn, tiled roof as they arrived, armed with flashlights and nervousness.

Inside the house, the air was laden with a somber aura. Peeling walls and dusty furniture seemed to guard the dark secrets of its past. The group's leader, Alex, turned on a flashlight and smiled at his friends.

—Ready for a night of spine-tingling thrills?— he exclaimed, trying to hide his own unease.

The friends nodded, but their expressions revealed their internal fears. As the night wore on, unsettling sounds and shadows in the corners played tricks on their nerves.

—Did you hear that?— Sarah whispered, her voice trembling.

—Don't worry, it's probably just the wind, — Mike replied, attempting to maintain a brave smile.

But as darkness deepened, strange occurrences multiplied. Flickering lights, unintelligible whispers, and fleeting figures in the shadows began to haunt them.

—This doesn't seem normal,— Lily murmured, clutching Alex's arm.

Suddenly, a door slammed shut upstairs. The group gathered, their flashlights trembling in their hands.

—Should we leave?— Jenna asked, her voice filled with anxiety.

—We can't give up so easily,— Alex insisted, though his confidence was starting to crumble.

The friends ventured upstairs, where they found a dilapidated room. A sign covered the wall, reading, —We will never forgive.
—

A sense of foreboding filled the air as the friends exchanged worried glances. Mike stepped forward, trying to conceal his fear.

—It's just a nasty prank. Someone must have placed this here to scare us,— he reasoned.

But before they could continue debating, doors and windows began to slam shut violently. The atmosphere turned icy, and distorted voices filled the air.

—It's real! The ghosts are here!— Sarah screamed, on the brink of panic.

A shadowy figure appeared before them, eyes filled with anger and vengeance. It was the manifestation of the tormented spirits of those who had died in that house, determined to retaliate against those who had dared to invade their dwelling.

—I'm sorry,— Alex stammered, his voice trembling. "We didn't know what we were doing."

The figure advanced toward them, emitting a chilling whisper. The friends huddled together, paralyzed by terror and guilt. But at that moment, dawn began to light up the horizon, and the figure gradually faded into obscurity.

With the first ray of sunlight, the oppressive atmosphere lessened. The friends left the abandoned house, their faces pale but relieved.

—What was that?— Mike asked, filled with disbelief.

Lily looked back at the house with a pensive expression. —A warning that there are certain places we shouldn't venture into, even if we think we can defy the past.—

The group walked away from the abandoned house, carrying with them the memory of a terrifying night and the lesson that some secrets must remain in the past, or else eternal vengeance may be their price.

The lighthouse's lament

On a remote and desolate island, a solitary lighthouse stood like a sentinel in the night. Its light had guided sailors for generations, but it also concealed a dark secret that only the brave dared to uncover. A group of investigators arrived on the island, eager to unravel the mysteries surrounding the lighthouse.

As they approached, the wind howled around them, filling the air with an eerie aura. Mark, the group's leader, adjusted his coat and looked at his companions. — We're here to find answers. But remember, don't take anything lightly.—

As they explored the lighthouse, they discovered dusty records and ancient journals that revealed the history of the lighthouse keepers, sailors who had sacrificed their lives to keep the light shining in the darkness. According to the accounts, the deaths of these keepers had always been mysterious and sinister.

One night, while reviewing documents inside the lighthouse, the light flickered and suddenly went out. Darkness enveloped them, and Mark's heart raced. —This can't be good!—

They lit flashlights and hurried to the lighthouse's control room. Upon opening the door, they found the room filled with shadowy figures, transparent but clearly visible. The deceased sailors, with torn uniforms and anguished looks, were trapped in a kind of limbo, repeating the routine of turning the lighthouse light on and off again and again.

—My God!— Emma exclaimed, stepping back in horror.

The investigators were trapped between fascination and fear as they watched the endless cycle of the spirits. One of the ghostly sailors approached Mark, his expression filled with desperation.

—Why do they linger here?— Sarah murmured.

Mark cautiously approached one of the spirits. "Are you here by choice or by force?"

The ghostly sailor seemed to try to speak, but his voice was lost in the wind. The lights began to flicker again, filling the room with intense brightness before plunging into darkness.

—I believe they are trapped here by the duty they feel toward the lighthouse,— Mark said thoughtfully. —They continue to watch over the sailors, even in death.—

The spirits gradually withdrew, their figures fading into the twilight. The lighthouse regained its characteristic glow, casting a calm and serene light over the island.

As the group left the lighthouse, Emma looked back. —Do you think they will ever find peace?—

Mark nodded, gazing at the lighthouse with respect. —Perhaps, when they find a way to fulfill their duty, they will rest in peace.—

The island faded into the distance, but the story of the solitary lighthouse and its tormented keepers remained etched in the minds of the investigators. The lighthouse continued to shine in the darkness, illuminating both the coast and

the memories of the brave sailors who
had lost their lives but whose inner light
still endured for eternity.

The last photograph

On a sunny autumn afternoon, the photographer Alan strolled down the street, drawn by curiosity to an antique store. Among the worn objects and forgotten relics, he found an old camera that exuded an aura of mystery. He decided to purchase it and take it home, excited by the possibility of capturing the hidden history that lay behind its lenses.

After adjusting the camera and loading it with film, Alan decided to take a series of photos in his studio. He posed his model and began shooting, but as he progressed, something strange began to happen. In each photograph, a ghostly figure manifested in the background, its spectral presence accompanied by a chilling sensation running down Alan's spine.

As he developed the images in his darkroom, Alan saw with horror that the ghost became increasingly clear and detailed. It was a hooded figure with bright eyes, staring directly at him through time and space. —It can't be real, — Alan whispered, his voice trembling.

Determined to uncover the truth behind this mysterious figure, Alan began to investigate the history of the camera and the antique store. He discovered that the store had been a former photography studio in the 1920s, and a photographer named Daniel had worked there. It was rumored that Daniel had a dark past and had been involved in questionable activities.

One day, while searching for more information, Alan found an old photograph of the store in its heyday. In the image, he recognized Daniel standing next to the same hooded figure that had been appearing in his photos. The figure's face seemed equally shrouded in mystery and menace.

With the photograph in hand, Alan returned to the antique store, where he met the owner, an elderly, wise-looking man. —I need to know who this person is, — Alan said, showing him the photograph.

The old man sighed, gazing at the image with sadness. —That's Daniel, the former photographer. It is said that he was involved in dark practices, and his desire to capture the essence of death led him to invoke a vengeful spirit. That specter has been haunting the owners of the camera ever since.—

—What should I do?— Alan asked urgently.

The old man handed him an amulet and said, —Carry this with you when you take photos. It can protect you from the influence of the spirit.—

Alan followed the advice and took more photos with the amulet. As he developed the images, he discovered that the ghost no longer appeared in them. The spectral presence had been dissipated.

The ghost of Daniel, finally released from his cycle of vengeance, had faded away, allowing Alan to continue his passion for photography without the supernatural threat that had plagued him. In a dark corner of history, he had found the truth behind the face in the revelation and had helped a tormented spirit find its peace.

The haunted hotel

The elegant Hotel Delphi, with its majestic architecture and promise of luxury, was a coveted retreat for those seeking a peaceful getaway. A group of people arrived with hopes of finding rest and recreation, unsuspecting that the hotel's walls concealed a terrifying history. A past that, like a distant echo, threatened to return them to the shadows of the past.

—Wow, what an amazing place!— exclaimed Patricia, marveling at the opulent lobby as the group checked in.

—It's certainly impressive,— agreed Simon, filled with enthusiasm.

During the first few nights, things seemed perfect. But soon, strange whispers filled the rooms, shadows glided through the hallways, and objects moved without explanation. Small incidents that piled up, leaving the group bewildered.

—Did you hear that?— Mike asked, his voice tense as murmurs filled the room in the middle of the night.

—It's just sounds from the old architecture,— Lidia said, trying to reassure everyone.

But when spectral apparitions began to become evident, tensions escalated. On one occasion, Jenna saw a figure in period attire in the bathroom mirror, but when she turned around, the figure had vanished.

—I can't stay here any longer,— Patricia said, trembling with fear.

—We're letting paranoia get to us,— Simon insisted, though his own voice revealed his uncertainty.

On a particularly unsettling night, the group gathered in the lobby to discuss their situation. —This can't be normal,— Mike declared. —There's something sinister about this place.—

The hotel owner, an elderly man named Mr. Granger, approached them with a understanding look. —Perhaps it's time to face the truth.—

Mr. Granger revealed to them the dark history of the hotel: it had been built on an ancient cemetery, and the souls of those resting there had been disturbed by the construction. Since then, the place had become a magnet for the supernatural.

—What can we do?— Lidia asked, filled with concern.

Mr. Granger handed them some ancient amulets. —These amulets can help protect you. But you must also find a way to bring peace to the restless souls.—

Determined to confront the supernatural threat, the group ventured into the depths of the forgotten cemetery, where they offered prayers and honored the departed. As they did so, the shadows seemed to slowly dissipate.

When they returned to the hotel, the apparitions had disappeared. Mr. Granger smiled at them approvingly. —You did the right thing. Bringing peace to those who have been forgotten is a noble act.—

The group left the hotel with a sense of relief and gratitude. Although they had been haunted by the supernatural, they had also found a way to restore balance and allow the souls to rest in peace. The Hotel Delphi, once tainted by shadows, regained its brilliance, but now it was imbued with a story of redemption and liberation.

www.ingramcontent.com/pod-product-compliance
Lightning Source LLC
Chambersburg PA
CBHW051303160726
47994CB00003B/1295